THE
HAUNTED
HOUND

ANNE SCHRAFF

STANDING TALL MYSTERIES
BY ANNE SCHRAFF

Project Editor: Carol E. Newell
Cover Designer and Illustrator: TSA design group

© 1995 Saddleback Publishing, Inc.

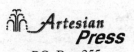

Artesian Press
P.O. Box 355   F-9
Buena Park, CA 90621
ISBN 1-56254-154-4
Printed in the United States of America
03 02 01 M 99 98 97 96   8 7 6 5 4 3 2 1

Chapter 1

Gerardo Hurtado hurried down the street with a book tucked under his arm. He had to finish *A Tale of Two Cities* tonight and write a report on it. He cut through the alley behind the deli and jumped over a fence. It was then that the other two boys jumped out, confronting him. "Hey, Gerardo!" the tall, beefy one taunted. "You got some money?"

"No," Gerardo snapped, "I'm not stupid enough to carry cash around here."

"Hey, man," the shorter one with the gap-toothed grin said, "you got a nice jacket there."

"It wouldn't fit you," Gerardo said.

He knew these two when they were harassing their classmates in fourth grade. Now they were bigger and meaner and they carried knives. And they had stopped showing up for school.

"The jacket would fit me," said the big one whose nickname was Caddy because the first car he stole was a silver Cadillac. "Come on, Gerardo, hand it over. I'd look much better in that jacket than a skinny wimp like you. I'd fill it out better, see?"

Gerardo looked around nervously. He wished there was someone on the street who could help him. But the one person he saw was a Vietnamese girl sweeping in front of the deli.

"Look, you guys, the jacket has my name on it and everything," Gerardo said, stalling for time.

Everyone called the shorter one Slider because when he wasn't ripping people off he raced around on a skateboard. Now he stepped closer to Gerardo, something silvery flashing in the darkness. "Hand over the jacket, man!" he said in a low, menacing voice. "There's two of us and one of you, and we got weapons."

Just then Gerardo heard a growl erupting from behind the garbage pails. A big dog with a black, silver-tipped coat and small, pointy ears stood beside Gerardo, his growl turning into a snarl. He was all red mouth and white fangs.

"Hey, where'd he come from?" Caddy gasped, backing up.

Gerardo watched in amazement as the snarling dog advanced towards Caddy and Slider. The pair wheeled around and scurried down the alley.

"Wow," Gerardo said, looking down at the dog who had suddenly turned friendly, wagging his tail furiously. "You sure showed up at the right time!" Gerardo said, kneeling down and taking the dog's head in his hands.

"Thanks, boy!" The dog's big, floppy tail thumped on the ground. "How'd you know those creeps were threatening me?" Gerardo noticed the eyes of the dog then—he had never seen such strange, luminous eyes on an animal before.

"I wish you could come up and stay in our apartment, boy," Gerardo said, "but pets aren't allowed. You wait right here. I'll get a treat for you." Gerardo ran up the stairs to his apartment and got some meat scraps from the refrigerator. Mom was still at work. She was the accountant at a department store.

"Here, boy," Gerardo said when he came back down. "I bet you're hungry, yeah! Boy, you saved me from losing my jacket! You're a great dog."

Gerardo went back upstairs to do his homework. He had to finish his English book report and tomorrow give an oral report on it. That's what he dreaded the most. When he got up to speak his voice usually cracked and his face got hot and red. He figured he had to be the shyest kid at Adams High.

Just before Mom got home, Gerardo went back downstairs to check on the dog. His gaze searched the darkness in vain. The dog was gone.

Chapter 2

Gerardo went back upstairs and turned on the oven for the casserole Mom left in the refrigerator. She was usually home around seven-thirty.

Gerardo thought about his Dad, how on a warm night like this he and his Dad would be outside shooting hoops. They both loved basketball. Dad was a lot of fun and Gerardo sure missed him. He couldn't believe it when that drunk driver came around a corner and squashed Dad's car like a grape. It seemed so awful, so unfair. Dad was such a good guy, working every day to keep his family going. Then some reckless jerk—some creep like Caddy and Slider—had to mess up everything.

Gerardo shrugged and went to the mirror. His teacher said he should rehearse his oral report in front of a mirror so he'd learn to smile and be more natural. Gerardo now stared at himself, at his thin face and his thick, blue-black hair. He looked like he was scared of his own shadow!

"Charles Dickens wrote many stories," he began, "and they showed rich panoramas of society ..." Tomorrow, at this point, his voice would crack and his classmates would giggle. He just knew it! Gerardo would feel like his tongue had a knot in it. He'd make a big fool of himself.

Dad was such a good talker. He could tell long stories that would entertain the whole family. Everybody would be shaking with laughter. Even serious Aunt Consuela cried from laughing so hard. Dad was charming. "Why am I such a *bobo*?" Gerardo asked himself sadly.

If bullies like Slider and Caddy bothered Gerardo's friend, Raul, he would send them flying in all directions. Raul was no bigger than Gerardo, but he had guts. Now Gerardo made a fist with one hand and slammed it into his open palm. "What's the matter with me?" he asked the empty room.

The next morning before he left for school, Gerardo checked the alley for his heroic dog. He didn't really expect to find him and he didn't.

"Hey, Gerardo," Caddy called, "I see you don't have your big, mangy dog with you. Did the pound come and get him last night?"

"Get lost," Gerardo snapped. "Why don't you go to school, Caddy? Maybe you'd learn something."

"School!" Caddy laughed. "That's for kids and *bobos* like you. Hey, Gerardo, how much money you got?"

"None," Gerardo said.

Raul came down the alley then. The two boys often walked to school together. Caddy faded away when Raul appeared.

"Was that *cucaracha* hassling you, Gerardo?" Raul asked.

Gerardo was ashamed to admit he was glad to see Raul so he said, "Nah, he doesn't bother me."

"Because if he was, I'd fix his wagon," Raul said.

Gerardo's face burned with shame. He hated it that Raul thought he needed protection. He hated it worse because it was true.

Gerardo fixed his gaze straight ahead, trying to forget his embarrassment. Then he remembered the dog and he said, "Raul, did you ever see a big, sort of black dog around here with real weird silvery eyes?"

Raul laughed. "Nope," he said.

"Last night, when I was coming home, he befriended me. He was really huge. And could he snarl!" Gerardo said.

"Did he scare you?" Raul asked.

"No!" Gerardo yelled. "I told you, he was my friend!"

"Okay, okay," Raul said, "don't get mad."

But Gerardo was mad. And he was ashamed, too.

Chapter 3

In English, Gerardo dreaded his turn to give an oral report. A very pretty girl, Dulce Robles, sat in the front row. She was sympathetic and when Gerardo made a fool of himself she always looked sad. She didn't laugh out loud like most of the others. Gerardo almost asked her out a few times, but he always got too nervous to carry it through.

The guy before Gerardo gave a smooth report on his book. Ms. Lynch praised him lavishly. "That's how a good oral report is done," she said. "With lots of eye contact and not reading every word so we're all bored to death."

Super, Gerardo thought miserably. What a great lead in to his report.

"All right, Gerardo," Ms. Lynch said, summoning him to the front of the room. In *A Tale of Two Cities* people were executed by a huge knife called the *guillotine*. Gerardo couldn't have felt worse walking to the front of the room. It was as if he'd been going to his execution. But then, as he passed a window, he was startled to see the dog with the luminous eyes. The dog must have followed him to school. Now he stood outside, tail wagging, head cocked intelligently as if he understood Gerardo's misery.

Gerardo turned towards the class. Usually at this point his heart began to pound. His mouth dried up. All the faces of his classmates turned into sneering, grinning enemies.

Suddenly a voice from inside Gerardo was saying, "If you think *A Christmas Carol* with our old friend,

Scrooge, was all Charles Dickens ever wrote, think again...." The whole report flowed from him without a hitch and he saw surprise in the sea of faces before him. When he finished, they even applauded!

After class, Dulce walked out with Gerardo. "That was a wonderful report, Gerardo," she said.

"Thanks. I practiced a lot," Gerardo said, but he'd practiced as much before. It was the dog. Something about the dog had given him courage. He couldn't understand it, but there it was. Now Gerardo broke off a piece of his salami sandwich and gave it to the big dog. "Good boy," he said, patting the large head. "You brought me luck today."

"Is that the dog you were telling me about?" Raul asked.

"Yeah. See how his eyes are sort of luminous, like stars?" Gerardo said.

"No, they just look like regular dog

eyes to me," Raul laughed. "He's big though. He seems to like you, Gerardo. You always wanted a dog, didn't you? Remember when your Dad said you'd get one when you moved out to the suburbs?"

"Yeah, I remember," Gerardo said.

The boy who gave his oral report before Gerardo gave his, walked over. His name was Mike. He was always one of the guys laughing the loudest at Gerardo's embarrassing oral reports. "Hey, pipsqueak, how come you didn't mess up today like you usually do? You been taking speech lessons or what?" he asked.

"Stop calling me pipsqueak," Gerardo said.

"But that's what you are, Gerardo. Everybody knows that," Mike said.

Suddenly the dog began to growl softly and his dark lips rolled back, baring his teeth.

"Hey!" Mike exclaimed. "Who let

that mad dog onto the school grounds?"

"He's not a mad dog," Gerardo said. "Leave him alone. Just back off."

Mike nodded. "Yeah, sure, no problem," he said, as he hurried away. Nobody wanted to be near the dog when he looked mad.

Gerardo grinned and hugged the dog. "I'm going to name you Hero. How do you like that, boy?"

The silvery eyes seemed to glow with a new intensity almost as bright as the headlights of a truck.

Chapter 4

Gerardo was on his way home when he stopped at the small deli on the corner. "Hello, Mi Hien," Gerardo greeted the clerk. "How's it going?"

"Okay, Gerardo," she said, "except when boys come in and steal. They just laugh when I try to stop them."

"What boys?" Gerardo asked.

"From junior high—see, two of them are coming now. One tries to keep me busy selling candy and the other rips off things in the back," Mi Hien said.

Gerardo knew one of the boys. He was Slider's younger brother, Ace. He was almost as tall as Gerardo even though he was only fourteen.

"Hey, Ace," Gerardo said, "watch

those sticky fingers in here, okay?"

Ace looked at Gerardo and laughed.

Then there was a soft growl outside the deli. Suddenly Gerardo felt strong and powerful—in charge. "Ace, buy what you want and then go home. You understand? *Comprende*?" Gerardo said.

"Okay, okay," Ace said, quickly buying a package of gum. He and his friend had fear in their eyes as they hurried away. Gerardo grinned after them and patted Hero's head. "We're like a team, boy," he said.

"Thank you, Gerardo," Mi Hien said. "Thank you for standing up for me."

"Anytime," Gerardo said, swaggering from the deli with his own purchase. Dulce and another girl came from the other direction on their way home from school. Dulce never used to notice Gerardo, but now she smiled and said to her friend, "This is Gerardo. He's in English with me. This is my cousin, Anita."

"Hi," Gerardo said.

"Gerardo gave a wonderful report in English today," Dulce told her cousin. "It was so interesting."

"It's hard to talk in front of people," Anita said.

"Yeah, well, I finally got the hang of it," Gerardo said.

"Oh, Gerardo, you are suddenly so macho!" Dulce giggled.

"Yeah," Gerardo agreed. "I just chased some creeps who were ripping off the deli."

"My!" Anita said.

"See you in school tomorrow, Gerardo," Dulce said. As she walked away, Gerardo heard Anita ask, "Is he your boyfriend, Dulce? He's so handsome!"

Dulce giggled again. "Maybe," she said. "I wish!"

"Oh, wow," Gerardo said to himself. He looked down at the dog that came from nowhere to trot beside him again. "You've changed my life, boy. I mean, you're like magic or something."

When Gerardo and Hero got to the corner of the street, Gerardo hit the 'walk' button and waited for the signal to change. After the light turned to green he and Hero started across the street. Suddenly from around the corner came a sedan with a crumpled front fender, roaring towards them.

Hero lunged at Gerardo, hurling him out of the path of the careening car. Gerardo scrambled to his feet and screamed in horror as the car struck the dog, throwing Hero on top of the hood.

"Hero!" Gerardo cried, his eyes filling with tears.

The sedan roared away as the big dog tumbled back to the street. Gerardo saw the driver—it was Caddy. Gerardo would deal with him later, but right now he had to do what he could for Hero.

Gerardo was in the middle of the street with horns honking around him, but the dog was gone. Injured as he was, how could he have disappeared so fast?

"Hero!" Gerardo yelled, his gaze desperately searching the dimly lighted street.

Chapter 5

Gerardo searched for Hero for almost an hour. Then he sadly decided that the poor dog had crawled away to some secret place to lick his wounds. Gerardo walked to Caddy's house. He didn't know what he would do when he got there. He wanted to pulverize Caddy for hitting his wonderful dog and then speeding off.

"What do you want, man?" Caddy's older brother asked, opening the door.

"Where's Caddy?" Gerardo asked.

"Driving around. What's it to you?" the man snapped.

"He hit my dog and then drove off," Gerardo said. "We got a score to settle."

"Well, you're in luck then, 'cause there he is," the older brother said with a nasty smile. Gerardo could tell Caddy's brother expected to see Gerardo whipped good in the next few minutes.

As Caddy jumped from the car, Gerardo yelled, "You hit my dog, scum!"

Caddy began to grin, then laugh. Abruptly his expression changed. He paled and tried to get back in the car as Gerardo charged him. Gerardo grabbed him by his shirt front yanking him from the car. He hurled Caddy into the dirt. Gerardo was like a different person, on fire with rage-charged power.

As Caddy cowered, Gerardo ripped open the hood and began ripping engine wires loose. He bent and twisted everything he could find. Caddy loved his car more than anything. Trashing it was the best thing Gerardo could think of to do.

Gerardo never stopped to wonder why Caddy gave up so easily. Why did he let Gerardo mess up his car? Gerardo was still so grief-stricken about what happened to Hero. It didn't seem surprising to him that Caddy was so easily cowed.

But then, as Gerardo finally turned away from the car, he saw the dog standing near Caddy. Hero had been standing there all along, softly snarling, his strange silvery eyes fixed on Caddy.

"Hero!" Gerardo gasped, running to the dog and hugging him. "You're all right, boy!" Gerardo ran his hands along the silver-tipped coat, finding no bumps or sign of blood. He'd been unhurt by the terrible accident. His bright eyes shone like before.

"Get that dog outta here," Caddy said.

"You better not mess with us anymore," Gerardo said over his shoulder as he walked away with Hero. Gerardo broke into a trot and Hero bounded after him. It was dark now and the dog's eyes glowed like neon. Gerardo's affection for the dog turned to wonder. He didn't understand what was happening.

As Gerardo jogged home, he thought about his Dad again. They used to jog together on warm nights like this, Gerardo and his dad. Dad would point out the stars in the sky. He knew the names of all the constellations. "There's the Big Dipper," he'd say, "and look, there's Orion's Belt!"

"I see a bright star, Daddy," Gerardo had once said.

"That's Sirius, the dog star," Dad said. "That's part of a constellation named Canis Major. Do you know what that means, son? It means big dog!"

"I want a big dog, Daddy," Gerardo had said.

"Soon as we don't live in the apartment anymore," Dad promised. "Soon as we get a nice yard you'll have a big dog, *mi hijo.*"

Chapter 6

Gerardo's father was killed only a few weeks after he made that promise. Now Gerardo knelt down in the alley behind his apartment, and put his arms around Hero and said, "Are you my big dog? Are you from Dad?" Gerardo's voice was filled with awe.

Hero wagged his tail and looked up at Gerardo in a way all dogs look at their masters—with love.

The next day Gerardo decided he'd ask Dulce for a date. Everything was going his way these days. He finally had the courage. He had no doubt whatsoever that Dulce would say yes.

At breakfast Gerardo told his mom about the dog. "You know that big dog that's been following me around, Mom. A guy hit him with a car yesterday."

"Oh, no!" Mom cried.

"He's okay, Mom. He's fine. It's like it never happened."

"But maybe he wasn't really hit," Mom said. "Maybe it just looked to you like he was hit. He might have jumped out of the car's way."

"I saw him bounce on the hood of the car, Mom, but he's unhurt. You know, he's not really just a regular dog," Gerardo said.

Mom laughed. "Not a regular dog?" she asked. "You mean he's a ghost, a *fantasma*?"

Gerardo laughed, too. "Yeah, it's weird, huh? But that dog has changed my life, Mom. I was such a wimp I couldn't even give an oral report in front of the class. Suddenly there was that dog and I did really well."

"Oh, Gerardo, you were always strong inside. You just matured slowly.

Now you are almost a man and all your good qualities are coming out. You were like a little caterpillar waiting to be a butterfly, waiting to sprout your wings," Mom said.

"Maybe," Gerardo said. "But I'm going to strike while the iron is hot! I've been wanting to ask Dulce Robles for a date all year and today when I get to school I'm going to ask her out."

"Why do you want to go out with Dulce Robles?" Mom asked.

Gerardo shrugged. "She's the prettiest girl in class, Mom. All the guys notice her."

"Are you so shallow that you only consider how a girl looks, Gerardo?" Mom asked in a disappointed voice.

"Gimme a break, Mom," Gerardo said. "I've never had the nerve to ask any girl out. Last year I sort of hinted to Irma Lopez that we could go for pizza after the basketball game. She made a big joke about it with all her friends. I felt like going to school the next day with a paper bag over my head."

Before he left for school, Gerardo stooped and gave Hero a big bowl of dog food and a hug. "I wish you'd come to school with me, boy. This is my big day. I'm asking Dulce out. I sure could use some extra good luck."

Hero jumped up and trotted alongside Gerardo as he walked towards school.

Gerardo rehearsed how he would ask Dulce out.

"Dulce, I have liked you for a long time and—" No, that would focus on what a wimp he had been in the past or why hadn't he asked her out before?

"Dulce, would you maybe like to go out with me? I know a good movie and afterwards we could go to that nice little Chinese restaurant they just opened up—" No, that sounded too much like begging, like Dulce would only go out with him if a great date was offered.

"There she is, Hero," Gerardo said, seeing Dulce and Anita under a pepper tree on the Adams' campus.

Chapter 7

"Hey, Dulce," Gerardo said as he approached the girls, "want to go out with me and have some fun?"

"Sure, Gerardo," Dulce said. "Friday's dance?"

Raul had been standing nearby and he said sharply, "Hey, Dulce, I thought you were going out with me!"

Dulce laughed. "You didn't exactly ask, Raul."

Gerardo looked at his old friend, Raul. "You never told me you guys dated," he said.

"Well, we don't. I figured she was going with me to the dance on Friday. I asked her if she was going with anybody and she said no. Then I said I'd like to take her and she didn't say no," Raul said.

Dulce suddenly glared at Raul. "Stop making a big fool of yourself, Raul. Gerardo is taking me to the dance, okay?" She walked over to where Gerardo stood and slid her soft little hand into the crook of Gerardo's arm. "Come on, Gerardo, let's go someplace else."

Gerardo felt a little bad to be taking Dulce away from Raul like this but it wasn't as if he planned it. Gerardo didn't even know Raul liked Dulce Robles. After all, Raul was a pretty serious guy and Dulce was a beautiful but silly girl. She didn't care about her grades and all she ever talked about were clothes and pop music.

At lunchtime, Gerardo saw Raul eating alone and he walked over to try to patch things up. "Hey, man, look," Gerardo began.

"Drop dead," Raul said, turning

away.

"Don't be a jerk, Raul," Gerardo said. "Let me explain."

"Don't sweat it, man," Raul said. "You and Dulce will be good together. You're both stupid and you both got no character. She dumps me in a hot second because she thinks she sees something better, and you steal your own friend's date."

"Look, Raul ..." Gerardo began.

"Can't a guy eat his lunch in peace without a creep bothering him?" Raul said.

Gerardo shrugged. "All right, man, have it your own way. I don't need you. I don't need anybody. It's all going my way now and maybe you're jealous. Yeah, that's what it is. I made a great friend as long as I was a pitiful nitwit. As soon as I get a little confidence and things start happening for me, you're jealous!"

Raul got up, his eyes narrowing.

"It's all that weird dog. He's put a spell on you or something. You're the same wimp you always were, but that weird dog has made you think you're some kind of superman. But think about this, Hurtado. Maybe someday that big old dog won't be there anymore. Then what're you gonna do?"

"Don't mess with my dog, Raul. Anybody messes with my dog is in big trouble, *comprende*?" Gerardo said.

When Gerardo got home that day he took Hero up to the apartment with him. He didn't care if it was against the building rules or not. He wasn't going to risk something happening to Hero in the alley.

"Gerardo!" Mom cried, seeing the big furry dog on the sofa. "You want to get us thrown out of this apartment?"

"He's my dog, Mom. He's saved my life and he's special," Gerardo argued. "Nobody is going to know if he sleeps up here with us."

"Gerardo, we can't have a big, dirty dog in this apartment!" Mom said.

"He's not dirty, Mom," Gerardo said.

"You want to break our lease?" Mom cried.

"If Hero can't stay, then I'll take my sleeping bag down and sleep in the alley with him," Gerardo yelled, shaking with emotion.

Chapter 8

"Gerardo! You're acting crazy!" Mom said.

"You don't understand! Nobody understands," Gerardo exploded. "Only Hero understands. That's because Dad sent him. He's the big dog my dad was going to get for me if he hadn't been killed. Nobody is going to get him away from me. Nobody!"

"Gerardo," Mom said softly, "it's all right. The dog can sleep up here in the apartment with us."

Hero was asleep on the rug in front of the television set when Gerardo went to bed that night. But in the morning he was gone.

"Mom," Gerardo shouted, "did you

put the dog out?"

"No, no, *mi hijo*," Mom said. "I didn't see him at all this morning. I thought you took him out."

Gerardo rushed around the small apartment searching for Hero. He looked under the beds and in the closets. "How could he be gone? The doors were locked. The windows were shut. How could he have gotten out?"

"I don't know, Gerardo," Mom said.

"Mom, he was my luck! My power! Without Hero I'm just Gerardo the wimp again!" Gerardo groaned.

"Nonsense! You are the same boy you were last night when the dog was here," Mom said crossly. "You are growing stronger and more confident. It is part of life. It has nothing to do with a dog!"

On his way to school, Gerardo searched everywhere for Hero. He whistled and called to him at every corner without luck. He finally arrived at school, more depressed than ever.

"Hey, Gérry," Dulce said, "you look sad. What happened?"

"My dog's gone," Gerardo said.

Dulce shrugged. "It was just a stray, wasn't it?" she asked.

"He was my dog, and I loved him," Gerardo snapped.

"Okay! Okay! Don't bite my head off," Dulce said. "It's just that I thought you'd be happy thinking about us going to the dance instead of all upset about some old stray dog!"

Gerardo turned sharply. "Don't you understand anything? This was a special dog. He was my friend. He saved my life when a car almost hit me. He was my best friend!"

Dulce's eyes flashed with anger. "A dog is a dog! You must be crazy to be making such a big deal about some old stray mongrel taking off again," she cried.

"I don't want to go to the dance

with you, Dulce," Gerardo said. "I haven't got the heart for it. You better go back to Raul!"

"I wouldn't go with you if you were dying to go," Dulce snapped. "If you care more for a flea-bitten dog!"

"Yeah, I do," Gerardo said.

Wonderful, Gerardo thought as he walked into his English class. His dog was gone for one morning and already his life was falling apart. He was reverting back to the luckless wimp he'd always been.

At the end of the day Gerardo walked slowly home. Then he heard steps behind him. "Hey, Hurtado," Caddy shouted, "heard you lost your dog."

"Yeah," Slider taunted. "Maybe he got picked up by the dog catcher and now he's history!"

"Poor doggy," Caddy laughed.

Gerardo turned and faced the pair who'd been making his life miserable since fourth grade. He'd always run from them, except when Hero backed him up. But now, no matter the consequences, he would not run.

Chapter 9

Gerardo took several steps towards his tormentors. "Get outta my sight, you scum bags," he screamed, his balled fists swinging at the ends of his arms. "I'm gonna knock your heads together, okay? I'm gonna shove you head first into those garbage pails over there." Gerardo couldn't believe the force and fury that poured from his lips. Caddy and Slider drew back.

"His eyes," Caddy mumbled, "they're crazy!"

"Meanest, wildest eyes I ever saw," Slider gasped, drawing back.

Caddy and Slider disappeared from the alley before Gerardo's surprised face. Gerardo turned and looked behind him. Hero must have returned. Sure, that had to be it. It was the dog standing behind him that made those creeps take off. But the alley was empty. There was still no sign of Hero.

Gerardo continued towards home, puzzled. Once or twice he whistled for Hero, sure that the dog would come bounding out, but it didn't happen.

Gerardo started up the apartment stairs, but then he stopped to see Raul leaning against the building, his hands stuck in his pockets.

"Hey, man," Raul said.

"What's doin'?" Gerardo asked.

"Heard your dog's gone," Raul said.

"Yeah, I'm feeling really down."

"Hey, Gerardo, I'm sorry. I'm really sorry, *amigo.* I hope you don't think I wanted it to happen. I mean I wouldn't mess with a guy's dog for no reason," Raul said.

"I know that. It just happened," Gerardo said.

"Still friends?" Raul asked.

"Sure," Gerardo said.

"Dulce decided she wanted to go out with me after you changed your mind about taking her, Gerardo," Raul said.

"Well, you going?" Gerardo asked.

"Nah. That girl is too much like a ping pong ball for me. Every time she sees a guy who looks interesting she bounces his way, but before he can grab her, she's bouncing off somewhere else," Raul said.

"Yeah," Gerardo said. "She's okay, but I don't think I like her much."

The next day in History, Gerardo had to give another oral report. He dreaded having to talk about the Puritans, but he'd put a lot of work into the report. He wanted to prove to his teacher, Mr. Acuna, that he wasn't 'painfully shy' like Mr. Acuna told him once that he was. "It's a pity, Gerardo," Mr. Acuna had said, "you're bright and you could go far, but unless you conquer your shyness it will hold you back."

Now Gerardo stepped to the front of the room and faced the class. "The Puritans weren't like we think," he began the well-rehearsed report, "they weren't all drab and gloomy. They painted their houses bright colors and they often dressed in gaudy clothes...."

To Gerardo's astonishment, he got through the report easily. Mr. Acuna was smiling his approval. Gerardo glanced beyond the window. Was Hero out there, rooting for him? Maybe that's why he'd done so well.

But Hero was not there.

"You've grown, Gerardo," Mr. Acuna said. "It's very good to see. You are becoming a man. Strong, forceful!"

Everyone who knew Gerardo was thinking the same thing and said so. He was different from the shy, insecure boy he'd been for most of his life.

Chapter 10

Gerardo remembered what his father had once said. "When a boy becomes a man it's a special thing to see. I want to see that moment when my son becomes a wonderful man!" Gerardo was swept by sadness as he headed home from school. He had earned a B+ in English and the other kids had come to respect him. He wasn't being hassled anymore by people like Caddy and Slider, but still he was sad.

Something was missing. Gerardo had grown to look for and enjoy the big dog. Hero had become the dog Dad promised long ago. Gerardo wanted to pat the fuzzy head again and see the love in those big liquid eyes.

Gerardo went slowly up the stairs to his apartment. He opened the door and then he saw it, the small brown and white puppy in the box by the stove. "The landlord said it was all right to have a little dog," Mom said anxiously. "I asked him today. So I bought you a puppy and now you have him."

Gerardo said nothing. He crossed the room and looked at the puppy. It wagged its tail and looked up with big, soulful eyes. It seemed to say 'Please love me or at least like me'. But Gerardo couldn't. It wasn't Hero.

"You don't like him," Mom said in a disappointed voice.

Gerardo shrugged. "It's a cute puppy, Mom. Thanks for trying to help."

"But you don't like him ..." Mom said.

Gerardo walked over to the window and stared out. It was a warm, cloudless night. It was the kind of night Dad would say "I'm taking a walk, anybody want to join me?" And whatever Gerardo was doing, he'd jump up and say "Me, me!" Now Gerardo said, "I'm going to take a walk, Mom."

"Be careful," Mom said.

"Sure, Mama," Gerardo answered. He hadn't called her 'Mama' in a long time.

As Gerardo headed down the alley, the big, shaggy dog fell in step beside him. Gerardo's hand dropped to the thick fur. It felt warm and inviting. They walked together to the top of the hill where the bowling alley was. It was the best spot for star gazing. That's what Dad said many years ago.

Gerardo knelt on the sidewalk, his arm around Hero. "That's Sirius, the dog star," he said. "That's part of the Constellation Canis Major. That means big dog."

Hero barked as if he understood.

Gerardo hugged the dog one more time, his eyes filling with tears, then he let go of Hero. The big dog bounded away through the darkness. He faded, almost seeming to take flight and leap into the constellation above.

Gerardo didn't know where Heaven was. But he knew his father was there. Maybe Hero had gone there, too. Gerardo did know that Hero had been a gift, a strange, mysterious gift sent to him to help him in his own painful leap from boy to man.

Gerardo turned and ran back down the hill towards home. His heart was suddenly light. He raced up the steps to the apartment, hurrying in the door. His mother stood at the stove, her eyes damp with tears. Gerardo put his arms around her and kissed her cheek. "You look pretty tonight, Mama," he said. Then he went to the box by the stove where the small puppy waited for acceptance. He picked the puppy up and said, "His name is Canis Major, but we'll just call him Major."